THE MOUSE THAT SNORED

for Samantha Shaye

THE MOUSE THAT SNORED

BERNARD WABER

Houghton Mifflin Company Boston

Walter Lorraine Books

Once there was a quiet man
as quiet as a mouse.*
He lived in the country
in a very quiet house.

*As most mice,
that is.

The quiet man's quiet wife
padded about in slippers.
She never made the faintest sound
not even while zipping zippers.

They had a cat
named Mose,
who went about
on tippie toes.

Hush!
Be
still!

And a parrot
named Will,
whose only words were
"Hush! Be still!"

While Will on his perch
would usually stare,
Mose mostly slept
on a parlor chair.

The quiet man, the quiet woman,
the quiet cat and bird,
ate their dinner, sipped their drink,
and never spoke a word.

Nor would they dare eat noisy food
like crunchy celery, munchy radishes,
or a snappy carrot,
— not even the parrot

They ate instead,
stewed tomatoes,
mashed potatoes,
and puddings made of bread.

At bedtime
they switched off the light
and ever so softly
whispered, "Good night."

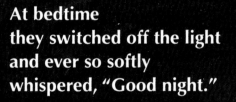

"Good night," said the man.
"Good night," said the woman.
"Good night," said Mose to Will.
"Hush!" said Will. "Be still!"

And silently they slept.
Not a cough. Not a sneeze.
The only sound heard
was the wind in the trees.

One stormy night,
while everyone slept,
into the house
a little mouse crept.

He was a city mouse
with city ways,
who was tired and hungry,
and had seen better days.

"Now for something to eat,"
said the mouse to himself.
And he quickly found food
on the pantry shelf.

"I hear something," thought the woman,
awake in bed.
"I hear something," thought the man,
raising his head.

"I hear something," thought the cat
in the chair.
The bird opened his eyes
and began to stare.

The mouse, now sleepy himself
and too full to eat anymore,
yawned, fell asleep on the shelf,
and at once began to snore.

And oh, what snores!

His snores were roars
with whistling encores.
And each snore was louder
than the snore before.

He snored
so loudly...

pots and pans
rattled and rumbled.
A freshly baked cake
immediately crumbled.

The light fixture
began to tremble and sway,
which startled the cat,
who kicked over a tray.

Glassware clinked,
dishes clattered.
A bowl from the cupboard
fell and shattered.

The lamp on the bureau
overturned.
Water in the fishtank
gurgled and churned.

Shutters flew open,
noisily banging.
A picture dropped
from where it was hanging.

Furniture danced
about the floor.
A parlor chair
went out the door.

And bouncing on his perch,
poor Will
frantically screeched,
"Hush! Be still!"

The snores were so loud...
the house began to quake.

The snores were so loud...
the mouse was shaken awake.

The mouse opened his eyes,
looked about in surprise,
and could hardly
utter a word.

For standing before
the mouse with the snore,
was the man, the woman,
the cat and bird.

Quick on his feet
and to break the ice,
the mouse said,
"Your house is very nice.

"And oh,
my gracious,
this pantry
is spacious.

"And I've never quite seen anything like this soup tur-eeeeeeeeen!!"

"Hush!" screeched the bird,
"be still!"
"Tell us," said the man,
"if you will . . ."

"Why you are here,"
said the cat.
"Yes," said the woman,
"please explain that."

"Very well," said the mouse,
"I will explain.
It was all because of that
cold cold rain.

"It was the storm
that drove into your house . . .

a lost

frightened

hungry

drenched to the whiskers

ever so tired

wandering homeless mouse."

"Ah," whispered the woman,
"how sad."
"Ah," whispered the man,
"it's really too bad."

"And now I will go,"
said the mouse.
"Sorry to have stirred up
this fuss."

"Nonsense!"
they cried,
"you will stay here
with us."

And so they took the mouse

HOME
SWEET QUIET
HOME

He was taught to speak
in a hushed whisper.
And to sound out his words
softly, but crisper.

To sit quietly
in his chair.
And never rattle
the silverware.

To make sure to laugh
in very soft chuckles.
And once and for all,
stop cracking his knuckles.

into that very quiet house.

One thing they taught him
that made him feel proud:
He learned to sneeze,
but not out loud.

KER-CHOO!

Soon it was clear
for all to see,
he was as quiet as a mouse
ought to be.

Except...

when he was asleep.

For then,
even louder than before,
the mouse continued
to snore and snore.

All through the house
his snores could be heard.

But not by the man.
— Oh, no!
And not by the woman.
— no, no, no!
And not by the cat or bird.
— no, no, no, no, no!

They slept peacefully
and cozily as bugs.

For now each goes to sleep wearing earplugs.